100 Mi
Writing Prompts

SCIENCE FICTION WRITING SERIES: BOOK 8

BY: KNATIA PARSON

Copyright ©2017 Knatia Parson

All rights reserved. No part of this book may be reproduced, distributed, or transmitted in any form or by any means, including photocopying, recording, or other electronic or mechanical methods, without the prior written permission, except in the case of brief quotations embodied in critical reviews and certain other noncommercial uses permitted by copyright law.

The writing prompts, contained in this book, are meant to inspire writers to create. The names, characters, places, and incidents mentioned in each prompt, either are the product of the author's imagination or are used fictitiously. Any resemblance to stories, writing prompts, actual persons, living or dead, events, or locales is entirely coincidental, and not intended by the author.

ISBN: 1977705944
ISBN-13: 978-1977705945

Table of Contents

Introduction

Introduction

After overcoming writer's block, I penned From Alien Invasion to Time Travel: 350 Science Fiction Writing Prompts, to help spark creativity, in fellow writers. Due to my interest in science fiction and a belief in helping others, I began a series of writing prompt books. Here is a list of previous books, in the series:

- Book 1: 100 Alien Invasion Writing Prompts

- Book 2: 100 Alternate History Writing Prompts

- Book 3: 100 Apocalyptic Writing Prompts

- Book 4: 100 Crime Science Fiction Writing Prompts

- Book 5: 100 Cross-Genre Writing Prompts

- Book 6: 100 Hard Science Fiction Writing Prompts

- Book 7: 100 Maritime Science Fiction Writing Prompts

The book you are currently reading is the eighth entry, in the Science Fiction Writing Series. Similar to my previous work, I have included 10 pages, for writing notes. I hope this, along with my other books, encourages you to keep writing!

100 Military Science Fiction Writing Prompts

1. Give an astronaut's account of a fight between alien soldiers, on the moon.
2. Describe the thoughts of a being who chooses not to reverse time, to prevent a war, on his planet.
3. Describe how a traitorous being is caught using astral projection, to obtain information, for enemy soldiers.
4. Describe what occurs as three, telekinetic officers, attempt to stop extraterrestrials from spreading poison, on Earth.
5. Describe the physical features of aliens, capable of sustaining an explosion, during a reconnaissance mission.
6. Describe the nature of a battle between soldiers, from Makemake and Ceres.
7. Describe how an officer, from OGLE-2013-BLG-031LBb, acquires the ability to melt the weapons of his adversaries.
8. Describe the largest warship, on Enceladus.
9. Create an otherworldly character, who is addicted to warfare. Describe his thoughts, as he is captured then, physically, incapacitated.

10. Vividly depict the perspective of a sniper, on Caloris Montes.
11. Describe events leading to the discovery of frozen soldiers, on Ganymede.
12. Write a backstory for a Neptunian scientist, who creates the illusion of a war, to drive humans insane.
13. Describe how the healers and inhabitants of a military hospital, on Kapteyn b, survive an attack.
14. Create a backstory for a nanoscientist, who becomes a soldier.
15. Describe why the leader, of an alien army, refuses to use robotics, to end a war.
16. Account for the abandonment of a large, military planet.
17. Describe what propels ground troops, on Dione, into space.
18. Describe why Venusians attempt to start a war, between Earth and Mercury.
19. Write about alien soldiers, who hypnotize their enemies into surrendering. Describe their fate, after encountering an army, who is resistant to hypnosis.
20. Describe how annihilating every bridge, on Kepler-1229 b, helps enemy soldiers win a war.
21. Describe events leading to the arrival of Plutonian officers, on Kapteyn b.

22. Describe why six, Venusian soldiers, defy orders to level Kepler-22b.
23. Describe how an occurrence, on Iapetus, leads to the development of a shape-shifting, weapon.
24. Account for the materialization of Martian tanks, on Earth.
25. Describe a military prison, on Ganymede.
26. Describe why using advanced warfare is forbidden, on TRAPPIST-1e.
27. Describe damage sustained to Neptune, due to excessive warfare.
28. Give a ground troop's account of a battle that halts volcanic activity, on Io.
29. Describe a scientist's revelation that officers, from Kepler-62f, have access to self-healing technology.
30. Describe how an injured, Plutonian officer, defends himself against Titans.
31. Describe the initiation of a battle, within a Mercurian fortress.
32. Account for the presence of a being, who revives fallen soldiers, abandoned in a battlefield.
33. Describe what occurs, after Europa's atmosphere is changed, to prevent human soldiers from landing on it.
34. Describe how an officer acquires a teleportation device, to catch a war criminal.

35. Describe what enables ground troops, on Proxima b, to aid an air defense, artillery unit.

36. Describe why a Venusian soldier is recruited to fight in a Martian war.

37. Write about a precognitive soldier, from Kepler-62e. Describe why he does not report an impending, military strike.

38. Describe a space explorer's revelation that military vehicles are being tested, on HD 40307g.

39. An extraterrestrial vehicle is destroyed, during a battle. Describe the reaction of a human soldier, as it begins to reassemble itself.

40. Describe how submarine warfare is conducted, in the methane lakes of Titan.

41. Describe events leading to the prohibition of verbal communication, during a battle, and why an extraterrestrial soldier violates this rule.

42. Describe how human soldiers prevent Titans from entering Earth's atmosphere.

43. Describe what occurs, as Neptunian infantry arrive, on Pluto.

44. Describe how the invention of a machine, capable of creating dark matter, initiates a war, on HD 100546 b.

45. Describe the method, in which, an extraterrestrial robot dismantles a laser cannon.

46. Describe how Uranian warfare causes temperatures to rise, on the planet.
47. Describe events leading to the addition of controllable, anti-gravity devices on military helicopters, to prevent them from crashing.
48. Describe how neuroscientist, on Jupiter, extract information from Venusian soldiers.
49. Describe why a Mercurian soldier speeds up time, at the start of a battle.
50. Describe how an otherworldly, con artist obtains military technology.
51. Describe why three, human ground troops, are abandoned, on Gliese 832c.
52. A Venusian, military unit perishes, on Mercury. Describe what an investigation, into the matter, reveals about its commanding officer.
53. Describe why humans go to war, for the inhabitants of Kapteyn b.
54. Describe how enemy soldiers suppress the telepathic ability of a general, from TRAPPIST-1h.
55. Describe the surface of Mars, after warfare causes the destruction of Olympus Mons.
56. Describe how beings, from Jupiter, construct a massive, space weapon.
57. Create a backstory for a Mercurian alchemist, who volunteers to fight in a war, against Martians.

58. Describe how a being flees a war zone, then escapes to a barren planet.
59. Describe why a Venusian volcanologist is forced to aid in a war, against Titan.
60. Describe how a soldier creates mountains, on a planet, to protect his military unit from heavy fire.
61. Describe an extraterrestrial army, capable of deconstructing tanks.
62. Describe why the presence of soldiers, from OGLE-2005-BLG-390Lb, suddenly cools down KELP-9b.
63. Describe an excavation, of Kepler-444 f, which uncovers advanced weaponry.
64. Describe how an intergalactic war causes a parallel universe to break.
65. Create a backstory for a combat medic, from Gliese 667 Cc.
66. Describe how creating a landslide helps Neptunians win a battle, on Pluto.
67. Describe what motivates a scientist, from Proxima b, to enhance the senses of a human soldier.
68. Describe the night stars begin to move, above TRAPPIST-1f, then reveal themselves as warships.
69. Describe how a Saturnian and a being, from Jupiter, help each other survive a battle, on Mars.

70. Describe what motivates Mercurians, Venusians, and humans to unite against soldiers from the moon and the sun.

71. Describe why a military unit, from Io, uses a device, capable of landing on Jupiter.

72. Create a backstory for a Saturnian inventor, who makes weapons for armies on Jupiter, Uranus, and Neptune.

73. Describe what causes a fighter jet to stop, in mid-air, during an aerial battle.

74. Describe how a battle caused the ejection of Cha 110913-773444, making it a rogue planet.

75. Describe the thoughts of an extraterrestrial soldier, who sees his death, but does nothing to stop it from happening.

76. Account for a broken alliance between Saturnians, Uranians, and Neptunians.

77. Describe the method, in which, humans attack Martian soldiers, during an eclipse.

78. Describe how inhabitants of Kepler-186f compress a warship, sent from Earth.

79. Describe what occurs, after voice recognition, laser guns, malfunction during a battle between Plutonians and beings from Jupiter.

80. An intergalactic war has ended. Vividly depict how a veteran builds a ship, on Kepler-296f, to return to his family.

81. Describe a fight between armed forces from Hat-P-11b and Jupiter.

82. Describe how underwater vehicles are used, during a battle on Ceres.

83. Account for the presence of a neural link between a soldier, from TRAPPIST-1b and a civilian, from HD 219134 b.

84. Describe why Kepler-37b is expanded, to serve as a military planet.

85. Vividly depict the physical features of extraterrestrial soldiers, capable of crushing their enemies' lungs.

86. Describe what occurs, as extraterrestrial soldiers break down the molecules of their human counterparts, during combat.

87. Describe what occurs, as telekinetic soldiers disable the cloaking devices of an opposing army.

88. Create a backstory for an alien scientist, who develops technology, to view war zones, on other planets.

89. Describe what causes Venusian weapons to backfire, in the middle of a battle.

90. Describe why Saturnian officers accelerate the orbit of their planet, during a battle against beings, from Oberon.

91. Describe a battlefield, on PSR B1620-26 b.

92. Describe how opening a portal, in space, helps soldiers on Kepler-138b win a battle against an army, from 51 Pegasi b.

93. Describe why beings, from Kepler-90h, are tasked with preventing a war, within their planetary system.

94. Account for the rise of induced, advanced intelligence, to win military battles, on Titania.

95. Describe what occurs after warships, from Proxima b, destroy Jupiter and its moons.

96. Create a backstory for a human, who develops hydrokinesis, to fight in a war against beings, from HD40307g.

97. Describe why a battle on Saturn changes the composition of Hyperion.

98. Describe how a fight, between Mercurians and Venusians, ceases life on Earth.

99. Describe why a shape-shifter, from Kepler-444 b, initiates a war with humans.

100. Describe a conversation between a human and a Martian, exchanging military intelligence.

About the Author

Knatia Parson is the author of From Alien Invasion to Time Travel: 350 Science Fiction Writing Prompts. She was born and raised in Chester, Pennsylvania. Her varied interests include astronomy, sociology, art history, and web development. Read more at Knatia's website: https://www.knatia.com/

Notes

Notes

Notes

Notes

Notes

Notes

Notes

Notes

Notes

Notes

28879351R10017

Made in the USA
Middletown, DE
22 December 2018